THE WORLD-FAMOUS BUNNICULA AND HIS PALS HAROLD, CHESTER AND HOWIE IN

RABBIT-CADABRA!

James Howe

Illustrated by Alan Daniel

AN AVON CAMELOT BOOK

To Betsy and Zoe –

Thanks for the magic

AVON BOOKS
A division of
The Hearst Corporation
1350 Avenue of the Americas
New York, New York 10019

Text copyright © 1993 by James Howe
Illustrations copyright © 1993 by Alan Daniel
Published by arrangement with the author
Library of Congress Catalog Card Number: 91-34656
ISBN: 0-380-71336-5
RL: 3.5

Published in hardcover by William Morrow and Company, Inc.; for information address
Permissions Department, William Morrow and Company, Inc., 1350 Avenue of the
Americas, New York, New York 10019.

First Avon Camelot Printing: March 1994

CAMELOT TRADEMARK REG. U.S. PAT. OFF. AND IN OTHER COUNTRIES, MARCA REGISTRADA,
HECHO EN U.S.A.

Printed in the U.S.A.

OPM 10 9 8 7 6 5 4 3 2 1

A Note to the Reader

The story you are about to read was written by a shaggy dog named Harold. Harold lives with the Monroe family and their other unusual pets: Chester, a book-reading cat; Howie, a fun-loving dachshund; and Bunnicula, a vampire rabbit—at least, that's what Chester says he is.

When Harold sent this story to me, he enclosed a note that read:

It doesn't take much to get things stirred up around our house. Some missing fudge, a birthday surprise—even simple things are enough to make my friend Chester suspect the worst. So you can just imagine what happened when a magician with a Transylvanian-sounding name pulled a frighteningly familiar rabbit out of his hat!

As usual, Chester's ideas led to trouble. And as usual, I was the one caught in the middle of it all! Still, I did learn a few things about magic.

Who says you can't teach an old dog new tricks?

If you love magic as much as I do, you'll enjoy reading Harold's story. And at the end of it, you can learn a new trick, too!

—THE EDITOR

It had been a long time since I'd seen Toby so excited—and all because The Amazing Karlovsky was coming to town.

"I can hardly wait for tomorrow night," Toby said to his brother. "Do you remember the last time Karlovsky was here?"

"It's not like I could forget," said Pete. "The only thing you've talked about since then is magic, magic, magic."

"You're jealous," said Toby. "You wish you were as great a magician as The Amazing Karlovsky. Or *me*."

He grabbed the wand his parents had given him for his birthday and held out a pack of cards. "Observe as I make the ace of diamonds rise magically from the deck," he said.

Pete snorted. "Big wazoo. Observe as *I* magically disappear."
And he left the room.

That night, Chester said to Howie and me, "Poor Toby's all worked up over some guy who pulls a rabbit out of a hat. He doesn't even know that the real magician in this house *is* the rabbit. That Bunnicula can get himself out of his cage like a regular Houdini *and* he turns vegetables white!"

It's true that Bunnicula is able to get out of his cage by himself. It is also true that the vegetables in our house turn white from time to time. I'm not sure how Bunnicula does the things he does, but Chester is convinced he is not only a magician but a *vampire*!

Of course, Chester does get a little carried away. For example...

The next morning, Chester, Howie, and I went out for an after-breakfast stroll. We'd gone several blocks when Chester suddenly stopped in his tracks.

"What is it?" I asked.

"There! On that telephone pole!"

Howie and I looked up.

Howie began panting nervously. "It's...it's..."

"It's Bunnicula," I blurted out. "But how could it be?"

Chester narrowed his eyes into tiny slits. "Do you remember the last time Karlovsky came to town?" he asked.

"No," I admitted.

"Exactly!" said Chester. "That's because we weren't here. The Monroes were expecting a houseguest who was allergic to dogs and cats, so they shipped us off to a boarding kennel. Only Bunnicula stayed behind."

"So what?" I asked.

"I don't know so what," Chester replied. "But believe me, Harold, when I do, you'll be the first one I'll tell."

I could hardly wait.

Later that afternoon, Chester woke me from a perfectly good nap to tell me he had it all figured out.

"I don't think it's Bunnicula on that poster, after all," he said. "It's a relative—a cousin, perhaps, from the old country. The name Karlovsky, it sounds Transylvanian, don't you think?"

I yawned. "Well—"

"And we all know what comes from Transylvania, don't we?"

"Coffee beans?" Howie piped up.
"Vampires!" Chester shouted.
Howie gasped.
"Follow me," said Chester.

"A magician from Transylvania who pulls rabbits out of his hat. And what *kind* of rabbits?"

"Transylvanian rabbits?" Howie guessed.

"*Vampire* rabbits!" said Chester. "This Karlovsky character is pulling vampire rabbits out of a hat. Think of it! There could be hundreds by now. We've got to stop him before it's too late!"

"But how?" said Howie.

"And where?" I asked.

Chester arched an eyebrow and said, "Elementary school, my dear Harold."

Chester kept to himself the rest of the day. I guess he was coming up with a plan—either that or keeping Howie and me from finding out he didn't have one.

Early that evening, the family burst into the room.

"How do I look?" Toby shouted.

Pete snickered. "You're only going to be in the audience," he said.

I woofed to let Toby know I thought he looked great—no matter where he was going to be.

"Okay," Chester said as soon as we heard the Monroes' station wagon pull out of the driveway. "The coast is clear. First, we need some garlic."

"Oh, goody," Howie said, "are we going to do some cooking?"

"Garlic," Chester explained, "stops vampires from carrying out their terrible deeds."

But in the kitchen, he cried out, "Oh, no! They're out of garlic. How can this be?"

"What about cinnamon?" Howie asked. "Or chili powder? Would those do?"

Chester glared at Howie and with a nod of his head indicated that we should follow him out the pet door.

"What luck!" said Chester. "There's enough garlic here to wipe out every vampire from Transylvania to Pennsylvania."

"But what a smell!" I said.

"Yeah," said Howie. "Maybe we should take the pepperoni instead."

Chester shook his head. "It's a well-known fact that pepperoni has no effect on vampires whatsoever."

Howie looked at Chester with awe. I didn't have the heart to tell him that what Chester doesn't know he makes up.

The school parking lot was full.

"How are we going to get in without being seen?" Howie asked.

"Or smelled," I added.

"Quiet!" Chester ordered as we slipped through an open door and crept down a dark, shadowy hallway. In the distance, we could hear the sound of applause.

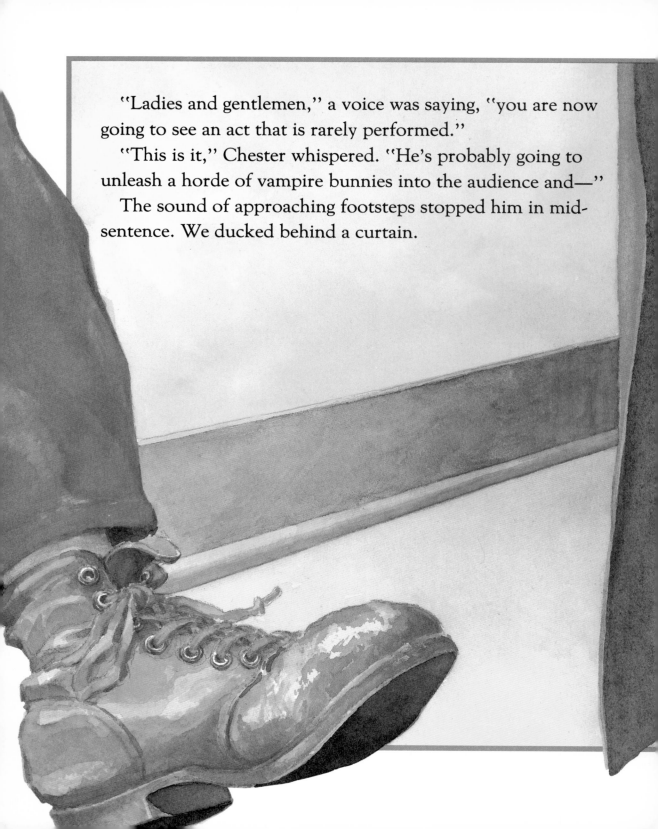

"Ladies and gentlemen," a voice was saying, "you are now going to see an act that is rarely performed."

"This is it," Chester whispered. "He's probably going to unleash a horde of vampire bunnies into the audience and—"

The sound of approaching footsteps stopped him in mid-sentence. We ducked behind a curtain.

"Phew," said Howie. "That was a close call."
We peeked out at the stage.

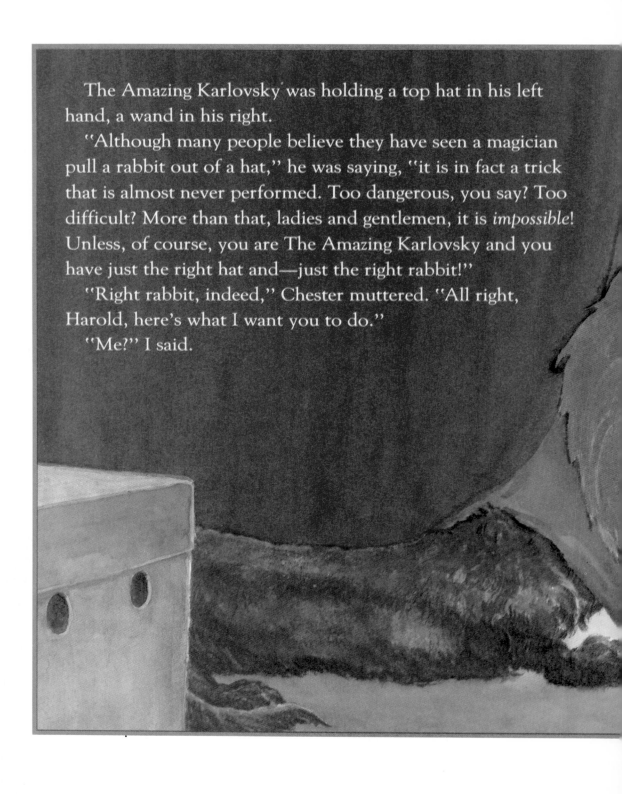

The Amazing Karlovsky was holding a top hat in his left hand, a wand in his right.

"Although many people believe they have seen a magician pull a rabbit out of a hat," he was saying, "it is in fact a trick that is almost never performed. Too dangerous, you say? Too difficult? More than that, ladies and gentlemen, it is *impossible*! Unless, of course, you are The Amazing Karlovsky and you have just the right hat and—just the right rabbit!"

"Right rabbit, indeed," Chester muttered. "All right, Harold, here's what I want you to do."

"Me?" I said.

Our conversation was cut off by The Amazing Karlovsky's booming voice.

"To make our rabbit appear, first we must get his attention. And what do rabbits love most?"

He held out a bunch of orange—

"CARROTS!" the audience shouted out.

Karlovsky waved the carrots over the hat, then lowered them inside. He circled his wand over the hat.

"Rabbit-cadabra! Appear!"

"Now!" Chester commanded.

I ran out onto the stage, the pizza clamped between my teeth.
The Amazing Karlovsky was amazed.
The audience went wild.

I tossed the pizza in the air, grabbed the hat, and raced across the stage. A rabbit jumped out, carrying a bunch of carrots in his mouth—*white* carrots!

The audience cheered and cheered.

The Amazing Karlovsky slipped on the pizza, just as somebody grabbed the rabbit and somebody else called out, "This is the best magic show I ever saw!"

And then the show was over. "Harold," Mrs. Monroe said, "enough is enough!"

"I'm sorry about what happened, Cousin Charlie," Mrs. Monroe said to the magician backstage. "I know you were looking forward to performing this trick for the first time."

"Cousin Charlie?" Chester whispered.

"Yes, I've always wanted to make a rabbit appear from a hat," said The Amazing Karlovsky. "I just didn't expect to make a pizza-delivery dog appear at the same time."

"I don't know what gets into our animals," Mr. Monroe said. "They act so strange sometimes. I wonder if it's something in their diet."

The Amazing Karlovsky sneezed.

"Oh, Charlie, your allergies," said Mrs. Monroe. "I think we'd better get them out of here right now."

"Cousin Charlie," Toby said as we were being led away, "I wish I could be a magician like you."

"Maybe one day you will be," said The Amazing Karlovsky. "Meanwhile, would you like to be my assistant at tomorrow night's performance?"

"Wow!" said Toby. "Would I!"

"Big wazoo," I heard Pete mumble. But I could see in his eyes that he was jealous.

"Well, Chester," I said that night after the Monroes were in bed, "what do you think of all your ideas now? It seems Charlie is Mrs. Monroe's cousin. *He* was the houseguest who stayed here before, the one who was allergic to dogs and cats. He used our bunny as a model for his publicity photo, which is why Bunnicula was on that poster."

"But why does he call himself The Amazing Karlovsky?" Howie asked.

"He didn't think The Amazing Charlie sounded very mysterious," I explained. "Karlovsky's a stage name, that's all. So, Chester, I repeat: What do you think now?"

"I think I'd like you to explain how the carrots turned white," Chester said.

We did not get to see The Amazing Karlovsky's second show. We heard that he pulled Bunnicula out of his hat without a hitch—and without a pizza.

Toby learned how the trick was done, but of course he isn't telling Pete.

Even Toby doesn't know how those carrots turned white, however. The Amazing Karlovsky himself says he's never seen anything like it.

But then—that was no ordinary rabbit he pulled out of his hat.

The "Rabbit-Cadabra!" Magic Trick
The Amazing Karlovsky pulled Bunnicula out of a hat.
You can, too. Here's how.

THE SECRET

After you make the HAT CARD, you will notice that the folded section forms a pocket—this is the SECRET COMPARTMENT. Gently squeeze the edges of the pocket and they will separate slightly. Now that you know where the SECRET COMPARTMENT is and how to open it, you are ready to start.

BEFORE PERFORMING

Assemble your props. Fold the HAT CARD so only the SECRET COMPARTMENT side is facing the audience. Hold the card as shown in **FIG. A.** Slip the RABBIT CARD under your thumb and hold it securely (**FIG. B**).

FIG. A

FIG. B

NOW YOU ARE READY TO PERFORM

1. Show the folded-together HAT CARD to the audience. Say something like, "Have you heard about Bunnicula, the vampire rabbit who sucks the juices out of vegetables? Well, I've heard he's hiding somewhere nearby. He might be as near as this hat—although it looks to me as if the hat is empty."

2. With your free hand, fold down the front half of the HAT CARD and show the unfolded card to the audience (**FIG. C**). Say, "Nothing is here." Be careful not to let anyone see the RABBIT CARD.

FIG. C

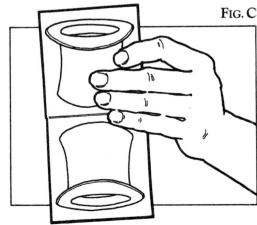

The "Rabbit-Cadabra!" Magic Trick was created especially for this book by Martin J. Schwartz, D.D.S. In addition to practicing general dentistry in New York City, Dr. Schwartz is an inventor and manufacturer of magic tricks.

3. Now grasp the bottom of the HAT CARD and fold it back and up so that the RABBIT CARD is wedged between the two halves of the HAT CARD (**FIG. D**). You should be holding the HAT CARD in one hand, as shown in **FIG. E**.

FIG. D

FIG. E

4. Squeeze gently at the top edges to open the SECRET COMPARTMENT. Then pick up the CARROT CARD and say, "Maybe he would like some carrots?" Push the CARROT CARD into the SECRET COMPARTMENT (**FIG. F**).

5. Pick up the MAGIC WAND and wave it over the HAT CARD saying, "Bunnicula, Bunnicula, please come out."

6. Lower the front of the HAT CARD toward the audience and say, "There's Bunnicula! And the carrots have turned white!" The RABBIT CARD will now come into view (**FIG. G**). Your audience will think not only that the carrots have made Bunnicula appear, but that he has turned the carrots from orange to white.

7. Turn your hand sideways to show that nothing is hidden on the other side of the HAT CARD.

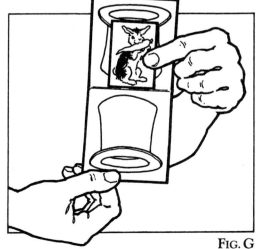

FIG. F

FIG. G

Turn to page 48 for the magic props.

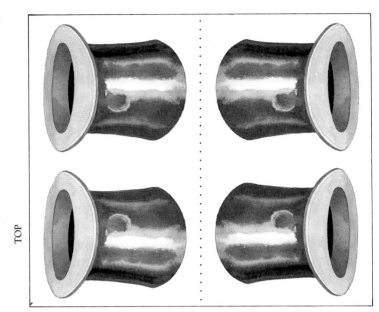

HAT CARD #1

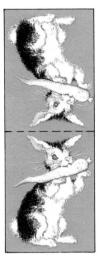

RABBIT CARD

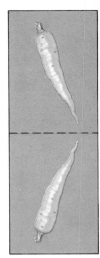

CARROT CARD

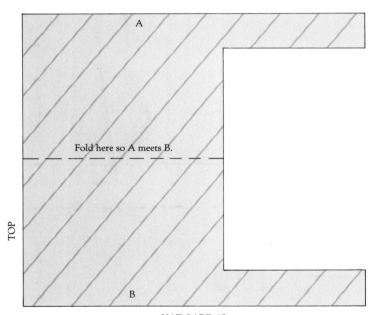

A

Fold here so A meets B.

TOP

B

HAT CARD #2

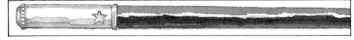

MAGIC WAND

Getting Your Props Ready

1. On a separate paper, draw or copy the pieces of the magic trick. You should make them bigger, but keep the same proportions.

2. Color the carrots in the CARROT CARD orange.

3. Very carefully, cut out the pieces along the **solid black lines.**

4. Fold the pieces of the RABBIT CARD and the CARROT CARD in half along the broken lines. Glue the two halves of each piece together with glue or double-sided tape.

5. With the illustrated sides facing out and the **top** part of each card facing up, glue or tape HAT CARD #1 and HAT CARD #2 together.

6. Fold the HAT CARD along the broken lines so that A meets B. Glue or tape the striped area together (use double-sided tape). Be careful not to get glue in any other area.

7. Fold the HAT CARD along the dotted lines.